Mature Woman Younger Woman Taboo Erotica

Lesbian/Sapphic Romance

Maureen Lester

TABLE OF CONTENTS

The Stranger

I could see that the woman was much taller than me, now that she was standing next to me. She ordered an Old Fashioned, her voice deep and sexy, from what I could hear anyway. As I internally battled with myself whether or not to try to start a conversation with the sexy stranger, she beat me to it.

She angled her body towards me, "Hello there," she said, leaning towards me a bit, so I could hear her over the loud music, although much of the sound didn't invade the bar area with how the place was designed.

She smelled good. Our eyes met again as I replied, "Hi." I gave her a bright smile, seeing her eyes flicking downwards to my red lips before looking at my eyes again, she smiled back.

"My name is Wanda, nice to meet you," she offered a well-manicured red hand to me and I took it, her hand enveloping mine as we shook.

Her grip was warm and sensuous just like the rest of her. "My name is Emily," I had to tilt my head upwards to meet her eyes. Our hands lingered before separating.

She lifted her drink to her lips as she looked down at me. I couldn't stop myself from glancing at said lips as I took another sip of my drink.

They looked succulent and it made me bite my own when the thought of kissing her lips entered my mind.

I immediately tried to think of other thoughts as I felt a blush coming on.

"Come here often?" She asked with a wry grin that said she knew how typical and basic the question was. It made me laugh and she smiled at the sound.

"No, it's my first time here," I spilled a little of my drink on my fingers when I laughed. I instinctively licked the droplets on my fingers and stopped when I saw her looking at my mouth with an intense look.

"Whoops," I said, a little embarrassed. Taking a napkin from the bar to wipe the alcohol from my fingers.

Her eyes felt like they were studying me like she wanted to know everything about me.

"I'm not from around here so it's my first time too, the hotel room was too quiet so I decided to check out the nightlife in the city," she told me as she placed her drink on the bar, "It's not my usual scene, a friend said they had good drinks and I didn't want to sit in my hotel room, so I thought, 'Why not?'"

"It's the same for me, my friends were talking about this place before so I thought it would be fun to come check this place out," I replied with a smile.

I didn't even notice I sidled a bit closer to her so we could talk better, she didn't seem to mind or notice either, both of us were mutually attracted to each other.

We talked and laughed, she especially loved it when she made me laugh, sharing tidbits of our life, who we were, how Wanda was much older than me by a little more than a couple of decades, and figuring out if the other one's single.

And we'd been flirting heavily, clearly, we both knew we were into each other.

We'd been making eyes, hers never leaving mine, exchanging heated gazes, my skin hot and I wanted to come closer and pull her in for a kiss.

Every time a part of us touched the other it was like

electricity coursing through us.

I'd never been with a woman, though I'd had fantasies for years of having sex with one. I didn't go there for a fling, but maybe a hot one-night stand with an equally hot lady was exactly what I needed that night.

Be brave, Emily, be brave, I told myself.

Wanda had been respectful and the way she talked and the way she listened to me made me hot all over. It was a turn-on that she never did anything untoward even though we'd been flirting hard.

Although at this point, I wouldn't mind. We were both consenting adults who wanted each other after all.

During a comfortable pause in our conversation, I finally got the courage to ask her for a dance. I finished my drink and got up from the stool I occupied and looked back at her, a come-hither look in my eyes.

"Will you come dance with me?" I asked, I felt the excitement in the pit of my stomach, and maybe a little dread just in case she said 'no'.

Wanda didn't make me wait long, she got up from her seat and moved close to me, and she leaned forward to whisper in my ear, "It would be my pleasure." And she took my hand and led me to the tessellating dance floor.

We moved our bodies to the music, the crowd around us doing the same, but our eyes were only for each other.

We moved towards each other, getting closer and bolder with each movement of our bodies until I could place my hands on her tits and look up at her with eyes full of desire.

I knew I shouldn't tease but this woman, with her feline smile, intense eyes, and sultry voice, did things to me. I was sure it was not the alcohol talking because I'd only had one drink.

With a graceful flip of my hair I turned away from her, moving my hips to the music as I pressed my ass against her groin as we danced together, the music thrumming inside us as we moved and teased each other.

She grabbed my hips with her long, beautiful, warm hands.

"Sweet Emily, you shouldn't tease a woman like me," she whispered in my ear, her nipples like hard knobs brushing against my back, and I shivered, but I didn't stop. Moving my head to reply, "What if I enjoy teasing you? What happens then?"

I heard her moan and pull me against her, she pressed her groin against my ass, and from what I had seen so far, she was very aroused.

She led us both to a darker section of the dance floor, her hands still gripping my waist.

"This happens," her voice an exciting hiss. She ground her

groin against me harder. She led my body through a heated dance, her hands exploring, getting bolder with each beat, stroking the skin not covered by my tiny dress, fingers trailing on the sides of my torso making my nipples harden under the glittery fabric of my dress, and she continued when I didn't stop her or pull away even when she paused for assurance.

Access Granted

One of her hands traveled down to the slit of my dress and didn't even hesitate as it arrived between my legs. My pussy was already getting wet with all the teasing I'd been doing and she was about to find out.

I didn't stop her long, slim, heated hands from reaching my lacy panties and moving the gusset to the side with her nimble fingers. I moaned at the feeling of her warm fingers, the loud music drowned it, I was sure nobody even noticed what she was doing to me under the darkness and colored lights of the club.

With Her long, slim, warm fingers rubbing against me, for the first time, I heard her inhale sharply next to my ear as she felt how smooth and bare my pussy was.

She felt my wetness too and without warning, pushed a finger inside me. I moaned loudly, unable to stop myself.

"You like that, huh? An older woman, a stranger, fucking you with her fingers in the middle of a crowded dance floor. You're soaking wet, Emily," I could hear the smugness in her voice and it turned me on even more coming from her, "A sweet and eager little slut, just taking what I give you."

I knew I shouldn't let her do this to me in the middle of a club, but I opened my legs further for her, my tiny dress riding further up my thighs.

She pushed another long digit inside me, "Fuck, you're

soaking my fingers. I feel you clenching around my fingers. I can't wait to feel you clench around my tongue later, to grind my pussy into yours. Would you like that? Or perhaps you want me to fuck you here?" She chuckled, her voice strained with want, "I just felt your tight pussy clench around my fingers again. You really are a naughty girl, my Emmy."

"My Emmy?" I thought I wouldn't mind being hers at all. I was already sure I'd let her do anything to me, I was so horny and enthralled.

Her dirty words and the slim long fingers inside me were the complete opposite of the lady she was when we were chatting mere minutes ago, and I loved it.

I was thankful for her arm firmly wrapped around me right then or I would've just dropped to the floor, my knees weak. My right arm raised, cupping the back of her lowered head and my left hand gripping the arm of her very busy hand was making me extremely wet.

To the other dancers, I probably looked like I was just sultrily grinding against her.

"I bet you wouldn't say 'no' if I ripped your panties and pushed my pussy onto yours right now. You'd take it like the good little girl you are and people will stare as I take your sweet cunt," punctuating her last few words with her fingers pushing deeper into me.

She seductively touched my neck with her lips, kissing me as I got lost in the feeling of her skilled fingers, "Maybe even let some of the other women pleasure you, all wet pussies taking turns giving you orgasm. I can tell you love being satisfied."

I let out another moan at the thought of being with multiple women at once, I'd thought about it once or twice before while I used my vibrator, I pressed my ass intently against her groin, and she chuckled, "Fuck me, you're a greedy little kitten, huh?" She rubbed her palm against my swollen clit and my hips jerked forward.

"Tempting as that is, watching you get fucked by other women, I want to focus worshipping your hot little body and hear your needy moans when I fuck you properly first," her dirty words made me shiver with lust, "And I especially want to see your beautiful face when I push my pussy up against it."

I felt my body shaking with intense need, my stomach fluttering at every filthy promise she whispered into my ear, "But maybe next time we can invite some people. Because there will be a next time."

She was so sure of herself and it thrilled me even more, I hadn't even experienced the whole thing and I already craved for the next encounter. How was that possible? I thought to myself.

"Come on my fingers, Emmy, and I promise you the most intense pleasure all night long in my hotel room, would you like that?"

I nodded at her offer with no hesitation, my back rubbing against her large tits as I moved.

"Say it," she insisted, wanting to hear my consent. A loud and immediate "yes" escaped my lips. Her fingers skillfully took me to the brink of my orgasm and she kissed me to swallow my moans as she rode my orgasm, my legs shaking, barely keeping me up.

Wanda held onto me as my body arched against hers, my hips moving of their own volition as intense pleasure shot through me.

"That's right, come for me," she whispered to me, kissing me on the neck and I threw back her head on her shoulder as I came down from my high. "You have a bit of an audience too. Some people are watching us, they saw you come undone, love."

That got my eyes fluttering open, but not enough to stop my body from throbbing with lust. It was a good thing it was dark and that Wanda moved us closer to the dark curtained walls of the room because I knew I was blushing from what just transpired.

I saw some people looking our way, including the bartender from before who was now eye-fucking me from afar.

I can't believe I let Wanda finger-fuck me to orgasm in public.

She didn't let me go though, she loved that I was with her and all these other bastards could just watch. But not for long because she desperately needed to fuck me.

She spun me around to face her, my hands resting on her boobs, a dazed look on my face as I looked at her. "I'm taking you home," she said, her voice thick with lust.

"Yes, please," I said, neediness coloring my voice.

Outside the club, it didn't take long for a cab to pick us up. Wanda gave the driver the name of the hotel, it wasn't far, but I could still cause just a little mischief.

I traced my left hand on her thigh next to me as I flicked my eyes to her to see her reaction. She was already looking at me, her eyes daring me to continue at my peril.

I moved further up until my fingers brushed her pussy lips through her short dress, I felt a bit of wetness there. I bit my lip, I couldn't wait to see it and taste it. Before I could tease her further she grasped my hand and entwined it with hers.

"You want to get punished, don't you?" Her voice was rough as she whispered to me, "That earned you some good spanking, little girl." I couldn't wait.

The short trip already had me squirming in my seat, Wanda had teased me, and whispered naughty things to me and she smirked as she watched me bite my lip as I tried not to moan in the cab and alert the driver of how intensely turned on I was.

I wanted to straddle her and grind myself on her without caring about the driver watching us, it was naughty and I never had that urge to throw caution to the wind with any man I'd been with.

When we got to the hotel, I expected a room but she had a whole suite!

"Would you like something to drink? Nothing alcoholic of course," she asked me. I gave her a questioning look, "I don't want you drunk. And I want you to remember everything we do tonight."

I bit my lip and I couldn't control the blush on my

cheeks at the older woman's words. "Just water, please..."

Just watching her catwalk to the fridge to get me bottled water shouldn't have been a turn-on but this woman did all sorts of things to my body, the butterflies in my stomach had been fluttering since the cab ride.

Thanking her as she opened the bottle for me and I drank half of it, feeling her heated gaze on me as I swallowed.

It was like she couldn't wait to get her hands on me and I felt the same, the delicious tension between us was palpable.

The moment I placed the bottle on the coffee table and faced her, our eyes met and we both stepped into each other's space. Wanda pulled me to her with an arm around my waist and one hand cradling my head as she kissed me passionately while I was kissing her back with the same fervor as I gripped her dress.

I moaned into the kiss as she tugged on my hair, angling my

head and moving her lips down the side of my neck, her tongue licking my smooth skin. I had never been this attracted and turned on by any guy I had ever been with, and we hadn't even had sex yet, at least sex in a "biblical" sense.

A mewling noise escaped my parted lips and I could feel her smile against my neck, "Already so needy for more, kitten?" She whispered in my ear, and her breath gave me goosebumps.

She was so close and she smelled so good. All of my senses were just overloaded by her, I couldn't help but nod in agreement, I didn't need so much more.

She pulled back, looking at me, my eyes half-lidded and my hands wandering down her boobs, trying to unbutton her dress.

She captured my hands in hers and kissed them, "Not yet." She could see how hard I was trying not to be impatient and it made her smile.

"Will you be a good girl for me?" She asked with that coaxing yet commanding tone that made me shiver with need, I leaned into her touch as she stroked my cheek. I nodded but she shook her head, "Tell me, little girl."
Why did her every command make me want to rub my legs together? Her voice was made to command me and I'd gladly follow. "I'll be a good girl...ma'am," I replied shyly, blushing as I added the last part, waiting for her approval. She smiled at her, "Of course, you will. And it's mistress, not ma'am."
I blushed some more, "Sorry, mistress."
She continued to stroke my cheek, then traced her thumb on my lips. I didn't hesitate to open my mouth to give her thumb a cute little lick.
Wanda could feel the painful throb of her clit in her soaked panties. This girl was intoxicating, thought Wanda. Every fiber of her being wanted to consume her and make her hers.

She watched me with intensity as I wrapped my lips around her thumb, licking and sucking it as my eyes met hers almost innocently. She pressed her thumb on my tongue, holding it there.

God, all the dirty things I could do with that beautiful mouth of hers, thought Wanda.

On Bended Knees

"Kneel," she added a little pressure on my tongue and I knelt without resistance, "So good at following orders, aren't you?" She removed her thumb, wiping the wetness on my lips and cheek, "Take off my panties."

I eagerly got to work, rolling the hem of her tight-fitting dress up to her belly. My mouth was watering already.

I couldn't wait to see her clit, to have my hands on her, and to taste her. I palmed her cunt and heard her moan, making me smile. She was not as unaffected as she tried to portray.

As I pulled down her panties, I could see her clit protruding from its hood. My eyes widened. I never expected a woman's clit to be that big.

I'd felt something on my ass in the club. But I had been so carried away I hadn't paid too much attention to it.

Her clit was thick and erect, protruding between her puffy cunt lips because of me. I leaned in, wanting to finally taste her.

But Wanda moved her hand to my hair and tugged it back, not enough to hurt, only to halt me.

"Are you hungry for my lovebud, little one?" She smiled down at me, I looked at her with pleading, hungry eyes, "Do you want to suck on it? Taste it?" I nodded fast, I had always loved oral sex, both giving and receiving, but I had never craved a man's cock as bad as I craved her pussy.

"Beg for it," Wanda told me, moving a hand to her clit and fingering it in front of me.

Wanda could see how badly Emily wanted it, she couldn't help but tease Emily, brushing her clit on Emily's lips.

She wanted to fuck Emily's face but she also wanted to take her time with Emily.

"Please, please can I suck your clit, mistress?" I begged, with desperation in my voice, I wanted to taste it so bad, I licked my lips just when she fingered her clit, "I want--no, I need to taste your clit, Mummy...please!" The words spilled out of me. My eyes flickered between her gaze and her pussy.

She cupped the back of my head tenderly, "Go on, please your Mummy," just as soon as she said that I wrapped my red lips around her swollen clit.

Wanda's head spun, and she gritted her teeth to stop herself from pushing Emily's head towards her and fucking her face.

She maintained her stance and her hand behind Emily's head, letting her explore her pussy on her own.

I moaned as I tasted her on my tongue, slightly salty yet sweet, just right. I alternated between licking and kissing her clit, not taking it wholly in my mouth yet, I wanted to tease her.

I encircled the clit with my tongue, it made my pussy clench at the thought of it pushing up against mine.

Watching her clit swell and looking up to see her reaction as I licked it, she looked at me like she wanted to pin me on the floor and devour me.

Taking her off guard I sucked her clit more aggressively.

"Fuck!" The outburst made me smile, or at least a semblance of a smile considering I had my lips around her clit, she gasped out the expletive and tightened her hold on my hair. That momentary loss of composure made me feel powerful, being on my knees with a mouthful of pussy, making my calm and collected lover swear and buck her hips. Wanda was breathing heavily, she moved the hand in Emily's hair to her chin, lifting it, "That is very naughty of you," she hissed, "But I can't say I don't enjoy it. So, suck, lick and eat my pussy, pretty girl."

With a pleased hum, I opened my mouth with my tongue out.

Emily was looking at her with those wide innocent eyes that pulled Wanda in at the nightclub as if she wasn't just sucking her clit a moment ago with her sinful red lips.

Wanda fingered her clit, then brushed it against the tip of Emily's tongue. "Keep your mouth open," she ordered.

She moved both her hands to hold my head, gently stroking my hair before she gripped it, and started fucking my mouth. With a whimper, my eyes closed in bliss at being used.

"Oh sweetie, that feels so good!" Wanda sighed happily as her hand gripped Emily's hair and pulled her harder into her sex, "Ohh, you're gonna make mommy cum. All over that pretty face of yours." As Her hand was so firm in Emily's hair, she couldn't help but take what was coming to her. Building closer and closer to her climax, she started to grind her pussy against Emily, rubbing her wet folds against her chin, mouth, and nose.

She was fucking herself against Emily's face and making a proper mess as she did -- which Emily started to enjoy. Her slick pussy lips spread wide open and smeared her tangy love juice all over Emily's face, coating her with her creamy love juice.

"Oh yeah, that feels soooo good!" Wanda groaned happily as she thrust herself back and forth, "your face feels so good, I'm going to cum all over it!"

Emily was a mess and loved it, being used in this fashion, helpless to be nothing more than an object for Wanda to use.

Emily's pussy was twitchy and wet but she didn't want to touch it yet. She wanted the honor to go to Wanda. All she did was kneel there and have her face used as Wanda's cunt tool.

Emily pursed her lips so that Wanda's labia spread over them and she was using Emily's nose to rub her swollen clit against, holding her head firmly and humping it like a dog against his teddy bear.

"Ungh, Emmy, yess, I'm going to cum!" she groaned loudly, her hips thrusting faster and her movements more urgent, "all over your Pretty. Little. Face!"

Emily was struggling to breathe properly, but there was nothing she could do except kneel there and be used. Wanda was grunting and moaning as she moved faster and faster, pulling Emily's face tighter into her drooling open sex, rubbing it across Emily's slippery chin and mouth, thrusting her clit against Emily's nose, and filling Emily's nostrils with her cum.

"Fuck!" Wanda cried out as she started to cum, her body shaking and her spread-open gash drooling and dribbling all over Emily's slick face, "Yesss!"

Her hands were tangled in Emily's hair and her hips jerked spastically as Wanda climaxed, copious amounts of love cream pulsing from her cunt and covering Emily's face, dribbling down her cheeks and neck.

Emily could feel her contractions as her pussy discharged more and more juice over Emily's face, until eventually she was spent, her hips slowing down and her hands releasing their grip on Emily's head.

"Oh Emmy, baby, you're a gem," Wanda sighed as she eased herself back and bent down, kissing Emily and licking up some of her juices, "that was amazing!" Then Wanda slipped on her panties. For the next few moments, Wanda busied herself cleaning Emily's face up a bit, kissing and licking her as she scooped up her cum and fed it to Emily, smiling as she stuck her slimy fingers in Emily's mouth and watched her suck them clean.

To The Bedroom

"I think it's time to move this to the bedroom," her sexy voice could make me do anything. I took her proffered hand and she helped me to my feet, my legs shaky from kneeling and also from the fact that I was so aroused.

"Thank you...Mommy," I told her as I wobbled a little bit on my heels.

"I should be the one thanking you," she chuckled, kissing my hand. For some reason that made me blush even after giving her an intense poon job.

She tugged me to her to give me a peck on the lips. She whispered, "Thank you, Emily. You can bring a woman to her knees with that delicious mouth of yours."

"You can't be real," I whispered incredulously, more to myself, before making up my mind and started leading her towards the bedroom.

I heard her let out a laugh behind me, obviously enjoying my flustered state and I felt my cheeks get hotter.

I stopped at the foot of the bed and before I could turn around I felt her hands on my waist and she pulled me to her, just like when we were dancing in the nightclub.

She brushed my hair to the side and started trailing kisses on my neck to her shoulders. I let out a breathy mewl and my eyes fluttered shut.

"Let me undress you, Emmy..." She murmured, moving one hand up my back to the thin straps behind my neck.

Wanda tugged at the ties carefully, unwrapping Emily like a gift. Emily could feel the top of her dress loosening on her body until it dropped to her feet leaving her in her pale pink lace panties and her strappy high heels.

Wanda's warm hands explored her skin, tracing her waist up to her bust where her long slim hands cupped Emily's breasts making her arch her back and press them against her palms, her nipples hardening again.

"Turn around and sit on the bed, pretty girl," she commanded me, kissing my bare shoulder before letting me go. I turned around and sat on the bed like I was told and I watched with rapt attention as Wanda slowly took off her dress.

Wanda started to unzip her dress, meticulously taking her time; she could see the hunger in Emily's eyes, as Emily licked her lips. Soon, the entire zipper was down, and she started to pull down the straps.

Once the dress had uncovered her breasts, she said, teasingly, "My eyes are up here," and saw her blush again which made Wanda chuckle.

Wanda could feel her pussy starting to get damp inside her black panties.

Then Wanda's hands slowly slip over her panties, covering her pussy. Even though I'd already seen her thick, long clit, I was still eager to see it again.

Wanda watched Emily, her lips parted and her eyes focused on Wanda's crotch. Wanda decided to tease Emily. She slipped her hand into her panties, pleasuring herself.

I licked my lips, eyes still glued on her panties, now with her playing with herself. "Do you want to see this again?" She asked me teasingly, fingering her pussy.

I nodded quickly, I wanted to crawl on my knees to her, to have my mouth on her pussy again.

"Since you've been such a good girl to me..." She chuckled.

She removed her panties and stood in front of me, I rubbed

my legs together, this woman was perfect. She took care of herself and wasn't afraid to show it. A lean and well-toned body, with large long nippled tits, I wanted to get my fingers on, hips asking to be ground into, I wanted to explore every bit of her.

My heart was beating fast and my pussy throbbing between my thighs. Every fiber of my being was attracted to her in every way.

Emily's lustful gaze on Wanda's body was interrupted when Wanda came closer and took her chin in her hand so she'd look up at her face, "I can see the need on your face," she bent down closer, "It's your turn now."

She kissed her softly on the lips, quite a stark contrast to the raging attraction inside both of them. My eyes fluttered open after the kiss as I wondered what she meant.

I didn't have to wonder long because she knelt before me as she parted my legs, with her expert hands she removed my strappy heels from my legs, massaging the marks they left on my skin along the way.

"As much as I want to fuck you in these sexy heels, we can always do that later," she gave me a cheeky wink. Her filthy words always made my pussy clench.

And then Wanda stroked Emily's legs upwards up to her panties, her fingertips tracing the edge of the lace, she pulled it towards her, and Emily lifted her ass a little so she could take it off of her completely, sliding it down Emily's smooth legs.

She looked at me as she pressed my panties to her nose and smelled my neediness before throwing them on the floor with everything else.

Now all our clothes lay forgotten as we stared at each other with hungry eyes.

Then Wanda broke eye contact to explore Emily's legs, kissing the soft skin of her thighs as she pushed Emily's legs open further. Emily helped her by parting her legs more, a blush already on her cheeks as she felt Wanda's hot breath on her skin.

Her face was so close to where I needed her the most. I watched her through half-lidded eyes, she was admiring me.

"When I felt this sweet bare pussy at the nightclub," her voice thick with need, her fingers stroking my inner thighs now, so close, "I wanted to rub my wet naked pussy against your wet naked pussy right then and there on the dance floor. I have never been so aroused like that, Emmy."

My name sounded sinful on her lips. She moved a knuckle to brush my already wet pussy lips and I instinctively moved my hips upwards to her which made her grin.

"I felt this urge to own this sweet little cunt, I didn't care if anyone watched me take you," she moved her head closer to the ache between my legs, her breath warm on my wet skin, "In fact, I wanted them to watch so they know you belong to me."

Her fingers tightened on my thighs and her words sent pleasurable shivers down my spine.

"Please, Mummy..." I gasped out, my body trembling with anticipation. I cried out when I felt her tongue swipe at my pussy lips, teasing me as I tried to lift myself to her mouth. But she put one strong arm on my hips to pin me in place.

"I--I need you..." keening sounds escaped my lips.

"Shh...patience, little girl," she chuckled as she pressed a kiss on my inner thigh, so close to my pussy that I felt her chin brush on my sensitive parts.

She purposefully moved slowly, kissing my legs and on top of my mound, drawing it out and teasing me. Then she put her mouth on my shaved cunt and started eating me out.

I screamed, if we weren't in such a huge hotel suite someone would probably have called the front desk to complain, but I couldn't help it.

My eyes almost rolled to the back of my head as I felt Wanda's skilled tongue pushing into my weeping pussy and her lips sucking on my sensitive clit. This woman was too perfect in everything she did.

I didn't even notice I fell back on the bed and my fingers gripping the sheets.

My hips tried to buck and my legs tried to close at the intensity of it but she pinned me open for her ministrations, my body arched from the bed, I felt so hot and already so close to another orgasm, her mouth felt so good on me.

Another scream burst from me as she pushed two fingers

inside me, my wetness making it easy to slide it in but my pussy still stretched a little bit to accommodate the sudden intrusion.

"Fuck, I can't wait to feel your pussy against mine, baby girl," she moaned as she looked up at me so delirious on the bed, "But I need you to cum all over my face first, I want to taste you."

She didn't let up, her fingers fucking me fast and rough, just like she knew I needed it. Then she removed her fingers to use her tongue and lips again.

"Oh fuck. OH FUCK! Wanda!" I didn't know what I was saying, all I could focus on was my orgasm, I felt like I was burning up, and then suddenly it was like I was falling,

I screamed again as my body convulsed, my pussy clenched and I started to cum, I could feel myself squirt as Wanda pinned my legs wide open as she slurped my juices.

When she let up and my body stopped shaking, I watched

her get up and sit on the bed next to my legs, her eyes still hungrily roved down my body as she licked the fingers that were just inside of me.

With a lazy grin, she beckoned me to her with her hand.

"Come here," she gestures with her hand and I shakily adjusted myself so I could crawl forward to her, my thighs slick with my orgasm.

When I was finally close to her she suddenly pulled me forward onto her lap, a squeal escaped my lips at the sudden movement.

"Did you think I forgot about your punishment, baby girl?" She bent down to growl next to my ear, "You think I forgot how naughty you were in the cab? How desperate you were for my pussy already? If I let you continue, you would've sucked my clit in there with the driver watching us through the rearview mirror."

I yelped as the feeling of two sharp hits from her palm to both of my ass cheeks registered.

I didn't regret it, I really would've, especially when I was already so turned on again, not even sure if I stopped feeling turned on this whole time. Another sharp spank pulls me out of my thoughts.

Wanda rubbed my ass softly, massaging me as I moaned, then she spanked me again, "That's for sassing me in the elevator when I wanted to know the dirty things running inside your pretty head."

She chuckled, "I think you're enjoying this, my Emmy."

Her warm hand stroked my bottom down to my wet cunt, her expert fingers stroked my bare pussy lips and I squirmed on her lap.

I kept rubbing myself on her. That got me a spank as well.

"Behave. You'll get my pussy when I say you do," she grunted, her voice thick with need. Wanda just wanted to pin Emily on the bed and fuck her senseless now, she was so quickly becoming an addiction.

"Fuck!" I gasped as her last spank was directly on my pussy, my body jerked and my legs closed tighter at the feeling. "That was for me, I couldn't resist this sweet weeping cunt of yours," she growled as she pushed two fingers inside to stroke me quickly before removing it.

She helped me sit up and kissed me hard, her fingers gripping my hair as our lips found each other. My hands gripped her shoulders, I loved the way she kissed me like she needed it to breathe. We parted and she helped me onto the bed, laying me on my back and pulling me to the edge of the bed, and propping my legs up on the mattress, wide open for her.

Emily looked up at her, her dark hair spread on the sheets, her lips parted, her breath panting in anticipation of what was next.

Wanda stood over her, her clit throbbing with need. She pushed her own hair back and was not sure how she managed not to just grind her pussy onto Emily's by then.

I slowly moved one hand to my pussy lips, stroking myself, enticing her, "My seductive little kitten," she cooed and smirked at me, "You want this on you, Emmy?"

She slipped her panties off, fingering her clit, "You want me to take you?"

I whimpered, "Yes, Mummy! Please, I need you to fuck me so bad. I've been thinking about it the whole night..."

I put two fingers on my pussy lips, opening my cunt to her, "Please! My pussy needs yours..." I needed to be fucked by her, I couldn't think of anything else.

"You're so pretty when you beg, how can I say no?" Her gruff voice indicated how much she wanted this too. She pulled me forward a little bit more, pinning my arms above my head and pulling one of my legs to hook her waist, then he guided her pussy between my wet lips. "Fuuuck...baby..."

It felt so slow, the way she pushed it against mine, I felt like I was going insane with the feeling of pleasure and impatience, my eyes fluttering close. As she pushed her pussy against mine, I felt my body trembling. I had never had anyone like her.

"Open your eyes, Emmy. Watch my clit on your tight little cunt, watch me own your little pussy," she grunted, gritting her teeth as she watched Emily's beautiful face.

I opened my eyes and had a hard time focusing but I did what I was told, "Such a good girl for me. Keep watching."

Pushing my whole lower body against hers as tightly as possible, I watched as she counter-attacked me the same way. We started a to-and-fro movement like we were a man and woman couple. We rubbed our clits as hard as we could, I didn't take my eyes off our pussies, watching them through half-lidded eyes. "Mummy...oh god..." My breathy moans filled the room.

"You make me want to lose control," she grabbed my waist, not wanting to let me go as she pushed further, a deep groan escaping her lips, "You feel so good and wet."

The sound of our pussies and our moans filled the room. All my brain could focus on was the ecstasy I felt every time our pussies pressed against each other "Oh god, you're so sweet..." I gasped out.

We pressed our crotches harder and harder against each other, we ground our pussies together like maniacs. Waves of ecstasy and pure lust were flooding all over our bodies. Our pussies attacked and counter-attacked each other, our clits fought. Two fighting cunts, that's what we were, nothing else existed in those moments.

Suddenly she dipped her head to kiss me. The kiss was hard and wild, just like how she was fucking me, our tongues dancing as we gasped and moaned.

When Wanda pulled back she watched Emily with dark eyes, Emily was writhing against her, so desperately needy, lips wet and parted, eyes hooded, and her hair messy. So perfect.

She put two fingers to my lips and I immediately opened my mouth to lick and suck just like when I had her clit in my mouth.

"You're still desperate for something in your mouth? You really are my needy little cunt whore, baby girl." She pressed her fingers on my tongue and I moaned in agreement with what she just said.

It was true, when it came to her, I felt all sorts of horny and needy.

"Look at you, fucking yourself on me as you suck my fingers," she growled, "I bet you'd be amazing to share. Have a girlfriend over or three, I can watch them fuck my pretty little slut, watch them take turns with you, or maybe we can all take you together, would you like that?"

She groaned as she watched me pick up speed, my body moving quickly on her pussy, chasing my orgasm.

"Fuck, of course, you'd like that, baby girl, because you're a wonderful cunt slut for Mummy. I bet you'd look so pretty having cum dripping out of all your holes after being used so well."

And at her words, I screamed around her fingers, my back bowed as my orgasm shot through me. Wanda removed her fingers from Emily's mouth so she could wrap a hand around Emily's throat. She watched Emily as her body shook with pleasure.

I was panting hard as I felt my orgasm take over me, it was so intense, just fucking myself on her as she told me so many sinful things, things I had fantasized about but never did. Wanda knew my body so well, the way she knew it would intensify my orgasm when she wrapped a firm hand around my throat.

After a few seconds, Wanda's cry filled the room as well. We rubbed our pussies together for a few moments more, then we separated. We were sweating all over, we almost couldn't breathe. We lay there together on the bed for a while, taking deep breaths.

Flipped Over

Then Wanda climbed off the bed and went under her bed, revealing a box of treasures. Emily patiently waited, sitting on the bed with her legs crossed, awaiting her next test.

Wanda picked something out of the box and showed Emily a strap-on cock that was about 8in long and 3in thick.

Emily watched, helplessly of course, as Wanda picked the strap-on and a bottle of lube, and carefully and thoroughly coated the whole length. Emily was wondering how her poor little pussy was going to cope with it -- she soon found out.

Next, Wanda greased Emily's pussy with the lube, two slick fingers opening her up "I think you're going to enjoy this Emmy."

Wanda started working the straps around her waist, fastening it tightly until the fake phallus was bobbing properly like a real one.

Wanda took Emily's hips and flipped her on her stomach. "On your knees, raise your ass for me, pretty girl."

And Emily did it without question.

I pulled my knees under me so I was kneeling, she raised my ass and parted my legs to open myself up to her. I can feel her eyes on me, watching my every move. I kept my chest on the bed and my thighs vertical as I arched my back and she stretched my hands in front of me languidly.

All I could hear was my breath and heartbeat, I knew she was still there watching, just taking me in. I didn't turn around, tried to be a good girl even though all I wanted to do was tease her and make her fuck me hard. I almost shuddered when I felt her approach and softly stroked my ass.

Wanda's entire body ached for her, seeing her like that, presenting herself for her to take was a sight to behold. It made her want to fall to her knees behind her and have her mouth on Emily's smooth pussy, to worship the beautiful woman.

But Wanda knew that was not what Emily needed at that moment.

Moving her hand downwards, letting her fingers caress Emily's wet and waiting pussy lips, she heard her whimper against the mattress.

"Tell me what you need, love," she told her as she moved to caress her ass, waiting for her answer.

She watched her let out a shuddering breath, trying to collect her thoughts. It's almost adorable how she tried to concentrate as Wanda rubbed a knuckle just between the lips of her cunt,

Emily pushed her ass towards her but Wanda just pulled her hand away, tsk tsk, she chuckled when she heard her whine.

"Tell me," she ordered again.

"I need it, Mummy..." I moaned as she brushed her knuckles on my sensitive clit.

"Need what?" She prompted.

"I need your cock!" I gasped out, keening noises escaping my lips.

"Tell me. I want to hear my little slut tell me what she needs..." with her free hand she stroked the arch of Emily's back, feeling her shiver with need.

She moved her other hand to the dick and stroked the bulbous head on Emily's wet pussy lips, up and down, before pressing her hips forward and the length rested between her pussy lips, never entering her, just grinding and coating the cock with her juices.

"I--I need your big cock inside my tight little cunt,

Mummy..."   Emily's desperation coated her words, "I need to be fucked like a good little whore, I need to be owned by you! Please take my pussy, Mummy! I need you to fill me up!"

It took all my strength not to push my hand between my legs so I could fuck myself.

I had never been this dirty with my past lovers, never this desperate and horny, but before I could contemplate it any further, Wanda took a hold of my waist and pushed the thick cock inside me to the hilt.

I was dripping wet but my pussy still stretched to adjust to the cock.

"That's right, baby, you need to be fucked like this, don't you? You need to be taken by a woman stronger than you, you need to be manhandled into submission."

Sounds of our skin moving against each other filled the room, our moans and grunts coalescing.

"You need to be pinned down and have your sweet bare

pussy take a large cock raw just like this!"
She pressed its length deep, hitting my cervix, and all I could think of was that it hurts so good.
"Yes! Yes! I need to be fucked like this! Just like that, Mummy!" I mewled, I felt so delirious with pleasure and need, my body sang for her like it never had with any other lover, but then my usual lovers weren't gorgeous older women who could pin me down and make me feel deliciously small and helpless.
My hands gripped the sheets, trying not to fall flat on the bed and keep my position.
Wanda bent forward, stroking down Emily's back and then to her head, gripping the strands of her hair with one hand, tugging a little, not enough to hurt her.
"Tell me what you're feeling, tell me how much you love this," she grunted as she slowed her pace but made sure each stroke was deep and hard.

"Oh fuck! Don't stop, Mummy! Oh god, it feels...it feels—," I gasped in agony. The cock hit me at just the correct angle, and I screamed. I felt another tug on my hair, a prompt that I needed to continue. I was trying so hard to think, to string words into sentences as the large cock filled my pussy.

"It feels so good! You're stretching me with your thick, deep cock!" I fumbled over it and moaned virtually every syllable, barely managing to keep it cohesive "I adore it. I love being used by you! I love being your little whore! Use me, Mummy!"

Wanda could cum just by listening to Emily beg to be taken, but she didn't want this to end just yet. She thrusted faster into her, not letting up, as she could see the telltale signs of Emily's incoming orgasm.

"What a good little whore for Mummy. You love being used, baby? Love having this big cock filling your tight cunt?" Wanda's voice was rough with exertion, "So good at taking my cock! So sexy, wet, and such a desperate little cock slut!" Her last words punctuated each thrust.

She snaked her free hand around me and started teasing my clit with her talented fingers. I felt like my body was on fire, her words, his voice, her everything, slowly pushing me over the edge.

"Mummy can see your pussy quiver, my slut, cum for me," she commanded me, my body quaking already, "Cum all over my cock! CUM!"

And I did, screaming on the mattress as the most intense orgasm swept through my body like a lightning strike, my body wanted to curl up at the force of my release but Wanda held me in position, keeping the rigid member deep inside my pulsing wet cunt.

"Such a good girl for Mummy..." She murmured, stroking my back gently, "So good at following orders and such an eager whore for me."

When I could finally breathe normally, she removed the cock from inside me. I almost whined but my brain was still fuzzy from my orgasm.

"Where--" I didn't even finish my sentence, she flipped me on my back again.

I enjoyed the feeling of Wanda's strong hands maneuvering my body, my heart picking up speed again and anticipation built in my stomach.

Her eyes were dark and focused solely on Emily like she was about to devour her whole as she knelt between Emily's legs.

Wanda took my legs and lifted them on her shoulders and then supported my ass with her hands. With a deep groan she entered her again, Emily's pussy immediately clamped down around the cock, still a little sensitive from her previous orgasm.

"Oh, oh!" I gasped out, my voice was raspy from screaming. "Please! It's too much! You fill me up so good!" I almost sobbed, I was babbling and delirious. She made me lose my mind.

"Take it, baby! Take what I give you, you need this cock, right?" she growled. "Like a nice little cock whore, accept it!"

I whimpered and moaned "yes", "please", and "Mummy" over and over, I felt so helpless to my libido and her.

I'd never cum so many times in just a few hours, but I could feel another one coming, I couldn't control my needy body.

"I'm so close, Emily," Wanda said through gritted teeth, the cock deep inside Emily, Wanda was ready to explode.

Wanda gripped her ass cheeks as she pounded into her, the other hand found its way to Emily's engorged clit, stroking and teasing mercilessly.

She was so close and wanted Emily to come with her.

"Cum with me, Emily," Wanda growled, each thrust pushing right to Emily's cervix, the cock so deep, fucking Emily like a wild animal.

With a scream, Emily's back arched as she threw her head back in ecstasy, "Oh god!" gripping the sheets around her as she thrashed as her fifth orgasm of the night took over, her pussy tight around the cock like a vice, "Please! Please, Mummy!"

The shaft of the shorter end of the double dong, tucked securely inside Wanda's cunt, had rubbed and butted against the stem of her clit the whole time she was fucking Emily, and the constant friction served to ignite an explosion of her own.

I heard her scream even as my heartbeat thrummed in my ears. Her hips bucked frantically against me but she held onto me tight, making sure the cock rested deep inside me.

My eyes fluttered closed and my body writhed in ecstasy, her arms still holding me up.

Wanda gently laid Emily's ass back on the bed, her body still quivering. She heard Emily weakly protest as she pulled out the cock and watched as

Emily opened her eyes to look at her, still kneeling between Emily's open legs, stroking the cock slick with her cum on her bare mound.

What's Next?

Wanda braced an arm beside Emily so she could lean down and stroke her face and give her a passionate kiss, gentle yet heated, Emily whimpered happily under her as she kissed her back.
"You love being my sweet little slut. You love it when I make you mine," Wanda murmured against her lips as she sweetly moved Emily's hair from her face with her fingers.
"I especially loved it when you made me yours at the club tonight. That was so naughty," I giggled at my new beautiful girlfriend. "You could have waited until we got here!"
"Waited? If I remember correctly, you were rubbing this delicious little ass on my

pussy first," Wanda chuckled as she smacked the side of my ass, "You couldn't wait, you were so horny that you let me fingerfuck you in public, and you came all over my fingers so prettily." She grasped my chin with her fingers as she smugly grinned at me.

I blushed at that, it was completely true, I got so worked up the moment I saw her. I pouted a little though, "Fine! But you made me horny, so that's not my fault!"

Wanda kissed her pouting lips and she couldn't help but smile, "It's unfair that my body knew you were near and that pleasure was bound to come next, especially my traitorous pussy."

Wanda tutted at her, moving a hand down her body to cup her pussy, stroking her pussy lips with her fingers. "Don't say that about my sweet obedient little cunt," she smirked at me as I moaned.

But she stopped before she could get me riled up again, we both needed to clean up and rest.

She kissed Emily's cute nose before pulling away.

She got off the bed and I watched her stretch her body like we didn't just have an intense workout in the form of mind-blowing sex, I didn't even think I could move right then, I felt like I'd been turned into a very sexually satisfied puddle.

She reached out to me and I shook my head, "I can't move anymore."

"Yes, you can," she laughed as she held my thighs and pulled me closer to the edge of the bed.

"No, you've completely wrecked me," I didn't move from my position and I felt her take both my hands in hers and tug me to her, coaxing me out of bed.

"If you don't get up now, you'll have to shower alone," she pressed on, "And I won't wreck you again after we get some sleep."

That got me to sit up from the bed and it made her laugh out loud. "Come on, my sex-crazed kitten." She took my hand and we both made it to the bathroom.

It was late by the time we finished. Wanda took care of me in the shower, washing my hair, my body, and my sensitive pussy still raw from our lovemaking.

I watched her clean herself up as I sat on the marble shower bench under the warm shower. It made me want to kneel and pleasure her again but I felt the tiredness settling on my body.

When we exited the shower she toweled me up, wrapping me in a robe.

Later in bed, Emily snuggled into Wanda's arms, happy to be with each other after two weeks of phone sex and sexting.

"I love you."

"I love you too."

THE END

• **Maureen Lester**